Dream Dogs

CHARLIE

16

With special thanks to Lucy Courtenay and Nellie Ryan

First published in Great Britain by HarperCollins *Children's Books* 2010
HarperCollins Children's Books is a division of HarperCollins*Publishers* Ltd,
77-85 Fulham Palace Road, Hammersmith, London W6 8JB

The HarperCollins *Children's Books* website address is
www.harpercollins.co.uk

1

Dream Dogs : Charlie

ISBN-13 978 0 00 732038 7

Printed and bound in England by
Clays Ltd, St Ives plc

Aimee Harper

HarperCollins *Children's Books*

Special thanks to

The Happy Dog Grooming Parlour, Farnham

Introducing...

Name: Charlie

Breed: Labradoodle

Age: 6

Colour: Creamy-white and brown (normally)

Likes: Being the centre of attention

Dislikes: Being left alone

Most likely to be mistaken for: A blueberry

Least likely to be mistaken for: A clipped standard poodle

One

Fire!

Outside the classroom window, Bella could see the sea glinting behind the playground. She rested her chin on her hand and stared dreamily at the view. There were just two weeks of term until the summer holidays. Soon, she and her mum, Suzi, her little brother, Louie, and their dog,

Pepper, would all be on Sandmouth beach, having picnics and ice creams and staying out late every evening. Bella hoped it would be a hot summer. It would be typical if the sun stopped shining in exactly two weeks' time.

"Bella?" said Mrs Frost.

Bella looked around in surprise. "Me?" she said.

Mrs Frost, the head teacher at Cliffside Primary, made a tutting noise. Mrs Frost had white hair and an icy gaze. The children called her Frosty.

"Yes, Bella," Mrs Frost said, raising her white eyebrows. "You. What ideas have you brought to the Summer Fair Committee?"

Bella tried to concentrate. She stared at the piece of paper in front of her. She'd drawn a picture of her dog, Pepper. It was a lovely picture. She was pleased at how she'd drawn Pepper's rough brown head and big dark eyes. But it wasn't very helpful right now. What had her class asked Bella to say?

"Well," Bella said nervously. "It's Cliffside Primary's fiftieth anniversary this year, and... um..."

The other children at the meeting giggled.

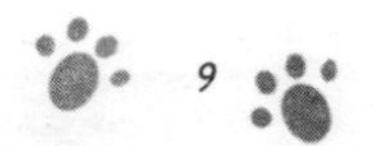

Mrs Frost sighed. "Yes," she said. "We know that. We have lots of things in place for the anniversary. But what ideas have your class had?"

It was no good. Bella couldn't remember. She was going to have to make it up.

"A dog show," she blurted out. "With... prizes for the waggiest tail, and... um... the smiliest face and... the wettest tongue..."

Bella knew she was rambling. But to her amazement, Mrs Frost started nodding.

"A lovely idea," said Mrs Frost. "We could charge a pound for people to enter. I shall bring my dog along."

Bella blinked. Mrs Frost had a *dog*? She'd

never seen Mrs Frost out walking a dog. It was a weird thought.

"What kind of dog have you got, miss?" asked Bella's best friend, Amber.

"A Labradoodle called Charlie," said Mrs Frost.

Bella frowned. She assumed Mrs Frost must have said '*Labrador*' and she'd just misheard her. She was about to put her hand up to ask, but someone called out, "A *labrabooble*! What's that?"

Before Mrs Frost could answer, Amber cried, "No, silly, she said '*dabydoodle*'!" and the whole class started laughing.

"OK, children, settle down," Mrs Frost said, raising her hand to get the class to be quiet. "Charlie is a Labradoodle, which is a cross between a Labrador and a poodle. It's quite a rare breed so it's no wonder that you haven't heard of it before."

Bella's mouth opened with surprise – she had never heard of such a funny-sounding name for a dog!

"You should bring Charlie to Dream Dogs one day, miss!" Bella said impulsively.

Mrs Frost looked puzzled.

"Dream Dogs is my mum's dog parlour," Bella explained. "We do washing and trimming and nail clipping and things like that. I'm sure Mum would—"

"Thank you, Bella," Mrs Frost interrupted, looking up at the clock above the board. "Can we get back to this meeting, please? The end of lunch bell is about to ring and I don't want you late for your classes. Any more ideas for the Summer Fair?"

Bella scribbled *Dog Show* on her piece of paper, underneath her drawing of Pepper. She felt excited. Imagine the school playing field covered in dogs, including Charlie the Labradoodle! They could use a loudspeaker to announce the results and have rosettes for the winners. Maybe Charlie would get one for being the most unusual breed! Bella couldn't wait to go on the computer at home and look up all about Labradoodles on the Internet.

The school bell started ringing.

"Back to class, everyone," said Mrs Frost.

Everyone headed for the classroom door, chattering about the Summer Fair. Bella glanced out of the window. She could see her friend Sophie, and her little brother, Louie, lining up to go back inside. It was a shame playtime was over. Apart from the grey cloud over the school hall, it was a perfect summer's day. Now Bella wouldn't be able to go outside until much later.

Bella looked at the grey cloud over the school hall again. And she realised it wasn't a cloud at all.

"Fire!" Bella shouted. She pointed. "The school hall's on fire!"

Everyone rushed to look. They could see flames shooting out of the hall roof. The smell of burning swept through the open window of the classroom. It made Bella cough.

"Oh, my goodness," Mrs Frost gasped. "Quickly, everyone. Outside!"

The fire bell started ringing loudly. Children jostled and pushed. Teachers shouted. Smoke was starting to drift down the corridors.

"No need to panic!" called Mrs Frost in a loud, clear voice as Bella filed towards the outside doors with everyone else. "Straight to your meeting points on the playing field, please! Everyone out! As quickly as possible!"

Bella felt scared. She'd never seen a proper fire before. The flames were rushing over the hall roof now. The sky was changing colour as the smoke began to blot out the sunshine.

The school had had a fire drill only last

week, so Bella knew where her meeting point was. For the first time, she realised how important fire drills were.

There was an explosion of sirens. Two fire engines screeched up outside the school.

Firemen scrambled for their hoses. Soon, fierce jets of water were dousing the hall roof.

Bella stood helplessly with her class on the playing field. She could hear some of the children crying as they watched.

Bella couldn't believe what she was seeing. Her school was burning down!

Dream Dogs on Wheels

"Mum!" Bella said feebly. "I can't breathe!"

"Did you breathe in too much smoke?" Bella's mum Suzi moaned. "Oh, my goodness, do we have to go to the hospital?"

"No," Bella gasped. "You're just squeezing me... too tightly!"

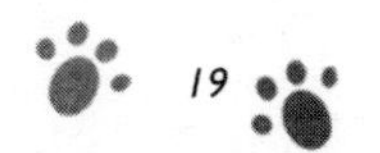

Suzi let go. Bella took a deep breath of fresh sea air. All over the beach, she could see parents cuddling their children. Pepper was barking and running wildly round in circles.

From here, it looked like the fire at the school had finally gone out. A mixture of steam and smoke still billowed around the buildings. Crowds of people stood watching.

"Oh, my life!" said Suzi. She gathered Bella and Louie in for another crushing hug. "When the school called, I thought my heart was going to stop!"

"Mum!" Louie grumbled, pushing Suzi off. "I'm not a baby!"

Suzi wiped her eyes. "You'll always be my babies," she said in a trembly voice. "Both of you. I can't believe this has happened! How did the fire start?"

"Don't know," Bella said. "The fireman are

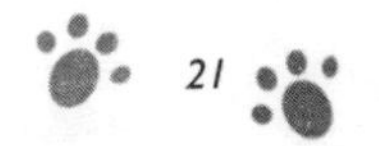

going to spend the rest of the week checking."

"Whoopee!"

Louie whooped. "Three days off school!"

"You'll miss football tomorrow," Bella reminded her little brother.

Louie's face fell. He was totally football-mad and he'd been playing in the school team since the start of term.

"They'll still do football though, right?" he checked hopefully. "We've got a match next week that's really important. It's going to be my first game and *I'm* going to be man of the match, not Jamie even though he's really good."

"I expect football will be cancelled too," Suzi said, and Louie groaned.

"Now," Suzi went on, "since I've got you a little earlier than expected, you'll have to come with me to my next job. I've got an appointment at the top of town."

Bella was confused. Customers came to Dream Dogs. Not the other way round. "You mean, someone from the top of town is bringing their dog to the salon?" she checked.

Suzi suddenly smiled. It was the first time Bella had seen her smile since she'd come to collect them off the playing field.

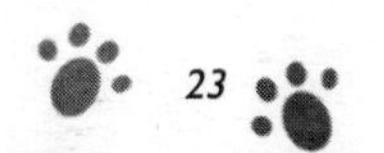

"I mean exactly what I say," Suzi said. "I've got a surprise for you both at home. I think we can all use a bit of good news today, don't you?"

Suzi refused to say anything else. Bella badgered her mum for clues. Even Louie was curious enough to stop grumbling about football and try to guess their mum's secret.

They came off the beach and walked

towards Dream Dogs. And at last, Bella saw the secret for herself.

Parked outside the dog parlour was her mum's Dream Dogs van. But attached to the back was a strange pink trailer. DREAM DOGS MOBILE DOG-WASH was spelled out in dark pink letters. In smaller letters along the bottom, Bella read: *Paws for Thought. The Pet Shop for All Your Pet's Needs.*

"I got the local pet shop to sponsor me!" said Suzi proudly as Bella and Louie rushed over to look. "They are helping me pay for it! Now I can take the business to all those people who can't come to the salon. People without a car, for example. Older people, and people with disabilities. Isn't it great?"

Suzi opened the back of the trailer. Inside was a bath and a shower unit, a tank of water and an electric pump. There was a cupboard full of towels. Another little cupboard held shampoo bottles. Both cupboards had lockable doors, to stop the towels and shampoos from falling out as the trailer drove along. Pepper jumped in and sniffed at the bath.

"It's brilliant, Mum!" Bella gasped.

"Come on then," said Suzi, checking her watch. "My appointment is at three o'clock sharp!"

They drove back towards the centre of Sandmouth. Smoke was still hanging over the school and part of the town was coned off. Bella saw some of her friends walking along the pavement with their parents. She grinned and waved. Her friends' eyes grew round as they saw the new pink Dream Dogs trailer trundling past.

Pepper put his head out of the window and barked.

He loved the feeling of the wind in his ears when they drove along.

"We need number twenty-three on this road," said Suzi, peering at the numbers on the houses as they took a sharp left. "There!"

Number 23 had a wide driveway. Suzi carefully backed the dog-wash trailer up the drive and put the handbrake on. As Bella and Louie scrambled out of the car, the front door banged open. An old man limped out. His hands were jammed in the pockets of his old cardigan. The top of his head was bald, although tufts of white hair were growing out of his ears. He was wearing a pair of sunglasses.

"Are you the dog-wash people?" he said gruffly.

Bella blinked. DREAM DOGS MOBILE DOG-WASH was printed in big letters on the side of the trailer. Of course they were the 'dog-wash people'. Then she saw that the old man was holding a small, folded-up white stick in one hand. He was blind!

"You must be Mr Flynn," said Suzi cheerfully. "Hello there!"

The old man didn't smile. "About time you turned up," he said. He called back over his shoulder. "Archie! Here, boy!"

A large German shepherd trotted outside. He had a big black body and a golden head,

and he sat down obediently at Mr Flynn's feet. He was wearing a special harness on his back, which Mr Flynn could hold on to.

"Is he your guide-dog?" Louie asked.

"What else might he be?" said Mr Flynn sourly. "My guinea pig?"

Bella frowned. The old man wasn't being very nice.

"Wait in the car, children," Suzi said. "I won't be long."

Feeling quite relieved, Bella climbed into the van with Louie and cuddled Pepper.

She didn't like the old man at all.

Three

Back to School

Bella and Louie sat in the car while their mum washed Archie, Mr Flynn's guide dog. They could hear their mum trying to talk to Mr Flynn as she worked.

"Archie's a lovely dog, Mr Flynn!"

Mr Flynn didn't answer.

"He's being ever so good. Most dogs don't like it when you wash their tummies."

Again, there was silence from Mr Flynn. Bella listened to the whoosh of the water from the water tank in the trailer.

"Have you had Archie since he was a puppy?"

"Had him three years," grunted Mr Flynn at last.

"You've been washing him yourself?" Suzi asked.

Mr Flynn snorted. "Couldn't see him to wash him, could I?" he said.

Bella glanced at Louie and pulled a face. Louie made cross Mr Flynn faces back, making

Bella giggle. Mr Flynn was the grumpiest man she'd ever met.

At last, the whooshing sound of water stopped.

"I can dry him if you like," Bella heard her mum say to Mr Flynn. "But I'll need to plug my dryer into your electricity supply."

"He'll dry in his own time," Mr Flynn snapped. "No need for that nonsense."

Bella watched through the car window as the old man handed her mum some money. Then, without a word of goodbye, Mr Flynn went back inside the house with Archie.

"He was a nasty man," Louie said when Suzi climbed into the van and started up the engine. "What a grumpasaurus."

"Yeah, he was mega-horrible," Bella agreed.

"Don't say things like that, kids," Suzi scolded. "We don't know anything about Mr Flynn. Your dad used to say, 'Walk in a man's shoes for a mile before you judge him.'"

Bella felt ashamed. She thought about what it would be like, walking in Mr Flynn's shoes. Mr Flynn had a limp, so walking was probably uncomfortable. And maybe lonely. It must be awful, not being able to see anything. Bella decided to be nice to Mr Flynn the next time she saw him. If he was grumpy back, she'd just look at his shoes and remember what her mum had said.

As Suzi turned the van and trailer out of Mr Flynn's road, Bella caught sight of Mrs Frost walking along the pavement. She glimpsed the back legs of a cream-coloured dog trotting beside the head teacher. *Charlie the Labradoodle!*

In all the drama of the fire, Bella had forgotten about Mrs Frost's dog, but now she remembered and desperately wanted to see what a Labradoodle looked like. She craned her neck eagerly. But Suzi accelerated and Mrs Frost and Charlie disappeared in the rear-view mirror.

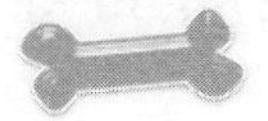

On Friday, everyone went back to school.

"But we only had two days off!" Louie moaned as Suzi helped him and Bella find their school books. "*And* one of those was football!"

"We should be grateful the school didn't suffer any more damage," Suzi pointed out.

"And no one was hurt, either."

"So which bits did burn down?" Bella asked curiously.

"The hall," Suzi said. "They have to rebuild the whole thing. The rest of the school was untouched, thank goodness."

When they reached Cliffside Primary, Mrs Frost was in the playground. Bella thought about Charlie again. Since seeing his back legs in Mr Flynn's road, Bella had been thinking about him even more than before. Who looked after him when Frosty was at work? Did Frosty have a husband? That was almost weirder than the idea of Frosty having a dog!

Everyone sat cross-legged in the playground.

Bella glanced sadly at the roof-less hall. It looked awful. Workmen were walking around the site, sifting through the rubble.

"Welcome back," said Mrs Frost in a serious voice. "We'd had a difficult week. But I'm pleased to say that everything is back to normal, as far as possible – except that assemblies will be here in the playground for the rest of term. As you can see, we have to build a new roof for the hall. And I'm sorry to say that this will cost over one hundred thousand pounds."

Everyone gasped. What a lot of money!

"We don't have to find *all* the money ourselves," Mrs Frost continued. "But our goal is to raise part of it, ten thousand pounds to be precise, and as soon as possible. I don't suppose assembly in the playground in December will be nearly as warm as this."

Bella looked at her best friend Amber. Was Frosty actually making a joke?

"And so," Mrs Frost said, "it's more important than ever that we make our fundraising fiftieth-anniversary Summer Fair the best one Cliffside Primary has ever had."

Back in Bella's classroom, Mr Evans handed out copies of newspapers.

"We have two weeks to put together a

special display for the end of term," Mr Evans told the class. "As you know, this year is Cliffside Primary's fiftieth anniversary. So we are going to do a project all about those fifty years, starting with today and working back to when the school was first built. Of course, we

now have to start by looking at our recent fire. I want everyone to read their newspapers and cut out any articles about the fire that you can see. They will make a dramatic start to our project!"

Bella settled down at her usual table with Amber and Sophie. They made their way through the papers, cutting out articles and taking turns to read them to each other. It was really interesting.

"The newspapers make the fire sound worse than it was," Sophie said.

"So more people buy the newspaper, I expect," said Amber.

Bella's eye drifted across the page of the *Sandmouth Bugle*. It stopped on a section marked "Obituaries". A name jumped out at her.

Clara Flynn, died aged 78. Much missed after fifty years together. My eyes and my heart, forever.

Flynn? Bella frowned. The bit about eyes... She was about the right age. And it might explain a lot about life in Mr Flynn's shoes.

Could Clara Flynn have been Mr Flynn's wife?

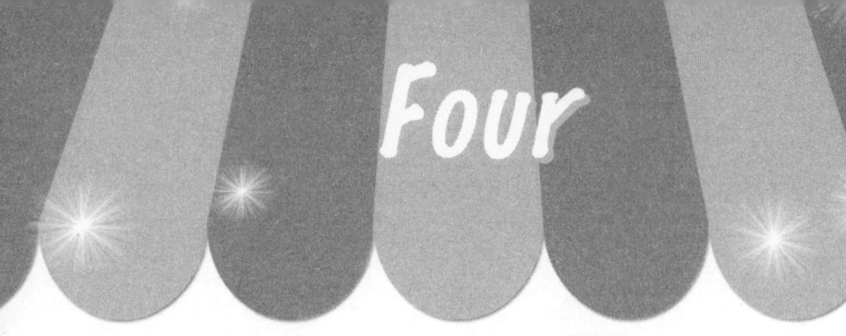

Four

Detention

"I would have done Archie's appointment earlier, but Mr Flynn wanted me at four o'clock," Suzi fretted as she collected Bella from school on Monday. "Thank goodness Louie has football after school today. Perhaps Claire will have you over to play with Amber."

"But I want to come," Bella said.

Suzi looked astonished. "I thought you didn't like Mr Flynn?" she said.

"I walked in his shoes for a bit," Bella explained, cuddling Pepper.

"Good girl!" said Suzi, looking relieved. "That makes my life easier."

At Mr Flynn's house fifteen minutes later, Bella helped to hold Archie while Suzi shampooed his broad black back. Pepper watched jealously out of the van window. He didn't like Bella fussing over other dogs. Bella could feel the question about Clara Flynn on the tip of her tongue. But Mr Flynn was scowling so fiercely today that Bella didn't dare say anything.

"Archie's been well looked after, hasn't he?" Suzi said, lathering Archie's back legs. "It's always good to see."

"That was my wife's job," said Mr Flynn abruptly. "Washed him every week."

"Oh!" said Suzi. "I didn't know you had a wife!"

Mr Flynn's scowl deepened. "I don't," he said. "Not any more."

Suzi looked embarrassed. Bella couldn't help it. She opened her mouth.

"Was your wife called Clara, Mr Flynn?" she asked.

Mr Flynn looked like he'd been struck by lightning.

"How do you know that?" he hissed. "Have you been spying on me?"

"I… I saw it… in the paper," Bella stammered. "I just wanted to say – I'm sorry…"

Mr Flynn shook his head. He lifted his hands to his face. To Bella's horror, tears were seeping out from under his dark glasses.

"There," said Suzi, pouring out two cups of tea. They were inside the house. Archie panted quietly at his master's feet. "We'll all feel better after this."

Bella sat in one of the armchairs. She stared at Archie. The big dog had guided Mr Flynn around a small table and sat down when they had reached the old man's armchair. She'd never seen a guide dog at work before.

"It takes getting used to," Mr Flynn said. "Not having Clara any more. I don't know what to do, really. I was blinded in the war, you know. We met years later. I never saw her face. But I knew what she looked like, all the same."

"Milk in your tea, Mr Flynn?" Suzi asked gently. "Where's the fridge?"

"Archie will show you," said Mr Flynn. "Milk, Archie!"

The big German shepherd got up and trotted into the kitchen. Suzi followed, with Bella close behind. Bella watched in amazement as Archie opened the fridge with his paw and set his teeth around the milk bottle's plastic handle.

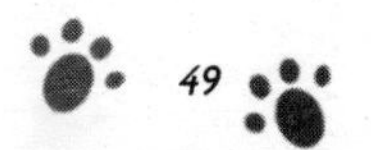

"You should bring Archie to my school one day, Mr Flynn," said Bella, as they came back into the sitting room and Suzi poured the milk into Mr Flynn's cup. "Maybe you could both come to our Summer Fair! Everyone would love Archie. He's so clever. I go to Cliffside Primary.

We had a fire. You maybe heard it on the news."

"I don't go out much," he said abruptly.

He got out of his chair and waved twenty pounds at Suzi. It looked like he suddenly wanted them to leave. Bella glanced nervously at her mum. Had she said something awful?

"Same time next week, Mr Flynn?" Suzi asked.

"Suppose so," said Mr Flynn. "You can see yourself out."

And the old man and his dog shuffled towards the stairs without looking back.

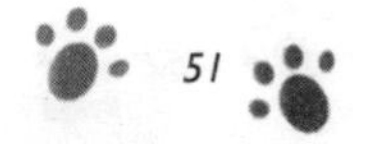

"I'm sorry, Mum," Bella said for the hundredth time as they waited at the school gates for Louie's football club to finish. "I just read about Clara Flynn in the paper and I wanted to know. He seemed really angry when we left."

"He wasn't angry," Suzi said, shaking her head. "He was just sad. Inviting him to the Summer Fair was kind, Bella. We'll ask him again when I go back next week. I think it would do him good to get out of that house a bit more. It would be good for Archie too."

"The paper said Mr Flynn and his wife were together for fifty years," said Bella. "That's as long as Cliffside Primary's whole life!"

Louie came towards them. He hardly

glanced at the workmen still picking over the site of the burned-down hall the way he usually did. He was looking furious about something.

"Whatever's the matter?" said Suzi in surprise.

Louie said nothing. He thrust a slip of paper at Suzi and stared at the ground.

"Detention?" Suzi gasped, staring at the paper. "Oh, Louie. What did you do?"

"It wasn't my fault," Louie muttered. "The football went much higher because Jamie bumped me just when I was kicking it and it

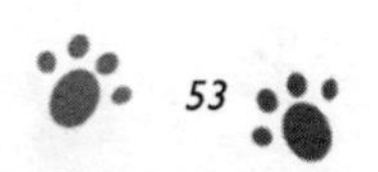

swerved through the window and then the glass wasn't there any more."

"You broke a window?" Suzi gasped.

"No," said Louie. "The *football* did. And I tried to explain it to Frosty but she just went mental at me!"

"Don't call Mrs Frost Frosty," said Suzi.

"Well, I WILL because she IS," said Louie fiercely.

"Did you know Mrs Frost has a dog, Mum? A Labradoodle." Bella said, suddenly thinking of Charlie. Although she'd looked at pictures of Labradoodles on the Internet, she still wanted to see one in real life.

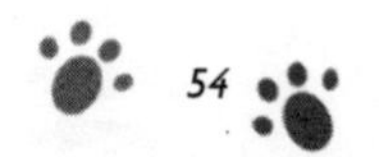

Suzi nodded. "I've met her on the beach with Charlie once or twice. He's a lovely boy. Really friendly and so unusual-looking!"

Bella felt annoyed. Why hadn't *she* seen Charlie yet?

"We're *supposed* to be talking about *me*, not stupid *labydooblies* or whatever they're called," said Louie, pouting. "I worked really hard to get in the football team and now I can't play!"

"When's your detention?" Bella asked.

"Next week," Louie moaned. "And I've got to miss my football match even though I've been looking forward to it since forever and I hate Frosty and it's NOT FAIR!"

Not Frosty At All

Louie sulked all the way home.

"It was going to be my first proper match," he said, over and over again. "It's so unfair, Mum! I hate Frosty and I don't care what you say."

Bella decided to stay out of things. When her

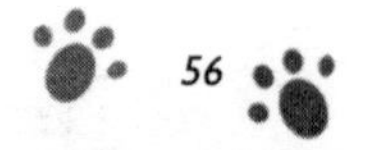

little brother got his teeth into something, he never let go. He was like Pepper with a bone.

"I'm not surprised Mrs Frost gave you a detention, Louie," Suzi sighed. "What did you think you were doing, playing football so close to the school buildings? As if Mrs Frost hasn't got enough to worry about!"

"Huh," said Louie furiously. "I'll get her back. You see if I don't."

He continued to sulk as they turned off the beach and walked down the road towards Dream Dogs. He folded his arms and huffed as Suzi opened the door to the salon. And he stomped off up the stairs to the flat as the phone beside the till started ringing.

Bella picked it up. "Hello, Dream Dogs?"

"Hello," said a familiar voice. "Is that Bella?"

Bella nearly dropped the phone. It was Mrs Frost.

"I'd like to make an appointment for Charlie," said Mrs Frost.

"Wow! That's so cool! I mean, um, yes that should be fine, Mrs Frost," Bella said, trying not to sound as excited as she felt. "I'll pass you to my mum!"

She handed the phone to her mother. She was going to meet Charlie the Labradoodle at last!

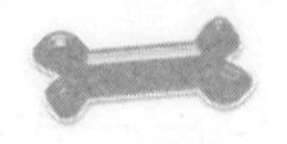

The next day, when Louie heard that Mrs Frost was coming to the salon, he looked like a thundercloud. Then he took a whole packet of biscuits out of the kitchen cupboard and disappeared into his room.

Mrs Frost's appointment was for four o'clock. Bella felt quite nervous as she changed out of her uniform and hurried down the stairs to the salon. She sat in the window seat with her arms round Pepper and watched the road. What would Charlie be like? And

would it be totally weird, having her head teacher in Dream Dogs?

Before she looked up Labradoodles on the Internet, Bella had thought Charlie would look like a poodle but bigger. The poodles she'd seen were clipped to look like the kind of bushes she once saw at a stately home. Bella loved the little clipped poodles, but privately she thought the big ones looked a bit silly, especially with those pom-poms on their legs. Although she'd only seen Charlie's back legs that time, she had seen at once that he wasn't clipped. She couldn't wait to see the rest of him.

At last, the upright figure of Mrs Frost appeared in the road. Charlie was trotting beside her on a bright red lead.

"He's *gorgeous*, Mrs Frost!" Bella gasped as Mrs Frost came into the salon with a tinkle of the bell. "Can I pat him?"

Mrs Frost smiled. "Of course," she said.

Charlie's brown and creamy-white fur was very soft. Bella loved the way the fur on the top of his solid head was curly, but his dished face

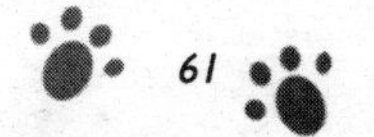

was smooth and only covered in short, fine hairs like a Labrador's. His ears fell like triangles, framing his clever-looking face. Charlie's eyes were very dark, and when he panted at Bella it looked like he was smiling. He stood as tall as her waist and had the chunky build of a Labrador. She hardly had to bend down at all to pat him.

Pepper sighed and trotted over to his basket as Bella fussed over the big dog.

"Charlie needs an all-over clip," Mrs Frost explained to Suzi.

"Not pom-poms," said Bella without thinking as she stroked Charlie's woolly coat.

Bella had never heard Mrs Frost laugh before.

"No, Bella," Mrs Frost said. "Not pom-poms. Although there's a good reason for cutting their fur that way. Like poodles, Labradoodles were bred as hunting dogs. Their coats were cut short on the body to make it easier for them to swim, and the fur on their legs was left long to protect their joints in the cold water."

Bella's eyes widened. She hadn't known that!

Suzi made Mrs Frost a cup of tea. Then Bella

helped to get Charlie into the bathtub. Suzi used a special shampoo for dogs with curly fur, and chatted as she soaped Charlie all over.

"Who looks after Charlie when you're looking after my children?" Suzi asked.

"I use a dog-minder," Mrs Frost explained. "Labradoodles aren't good at being left alone. They love company. It would be cruel to leave him at home by himself."

"You should bring him to school, Mrs Frost," suggested Bella. She took the shower head from her mum and directed it at Charlie's legs.

"I don't think I'd get very much work done," said Mrs Frost. "But I will bring him to the Summer Fair. Your idea about a dog show was

a good one, Bella."

"I've had another dog idea for the fair, Mrs Frost," said Bella.

Mrs Frost raised her eyebrows. Bella felt nervous. She'd been chewing over this idea for about a week now.

"Well?" Mrs Frost prompted.

"I haven't actually asked my mum yet," said Bella, a bit awkwardly. "And she's kind of important for the whole thing."

"My mind boggles!" said Suzi, turning off the shower head and throwing a towel over Charlie's wet back. "What are you planning, Bella?"

"I thought we could take the trailer and do doggy make-overs," Bella said in a rush. "Loads of people are bringing their dogs for the dog show already. I know kids in my class who'd love to help too. Maybe you could charge fifty pence if they wanted to help do the washing, and five pounds per dog or something?"

Suzi looked interested as she rubbed Charlie dry. "I'm happy to do it," she said. "What do you think, Mrs Frost?"

"Wonderful," said Mrs Frost. "It's a date!"

And to Bella's delight, she didn't look a bit Frosty as she said it.

Six

Clara

It was the day of the football match – and the day of Louie's detention.

"I'm ill," Louie shouted. "I'm not going to school."

Suzi put her arm round him as Bella dried up the breakfast dishes.

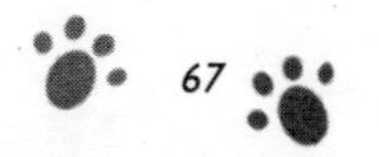

"There'll be more football matches," she said.

"Not first football matches," said Louie. "Not football matches when I'm the best from the BEGINNING."

Suzi looked at the clock. It was already eight-thirty. They were going to be late. "Well, if you're really that ill, Louie, then you definitely won't want your dinner tonight. Which is a shame as it's your favourite – home-made burgers and chocolate mousse for pudding." Suzi winked at Bella. "And there's no way you should play football for at least a week while you get better."

That sealed the deal and after the world's

loudest huff, Louie picked up his school bag and headed towards the door. "Come on then, slowcoaches," he teased.

They all walked down the beach together. Bella pulled her coat a little closer. The wind off the sea was strong. Pepper's fur was being blown in lots of different directions.

"How's your 'Fifty Years' project coming along?" Suzi asked Bella as they walked along.

"It's good," said Bella enthusiastically. Before they started the project, she had never known history could be so interesting. "We've been working backwards from today to when Cliffside first started. Last lesson, we found old newspaper articles about the rubbish that got piled up in the school grounds when the rubbish collectors went on strike thirty years ago!"

"It must have smelled horrible," said Suzi with a shudder.

"Pepper would have enjoyed it," Bella said cheerfully. "He loves stinky things."

She kissed her mum goodbye at the gates

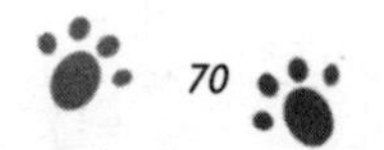

and ruffled Pepper's fur. Then she and Louie went inside to their lessons.

Bella's 'Fifty Years' project was nearly finished.

"I've got lots of information for us to read about the year Cliffside was built," Mr Evans told everyone that afternoon. "They dug up all kinds of interesting things when they laid the foundations."

"Did they find any bones, sir?" joked one of the boys at the back of the class.

Mr Evans scratched his head. "Yes, they did," he said.

Bella and Amber shared an excited glance as

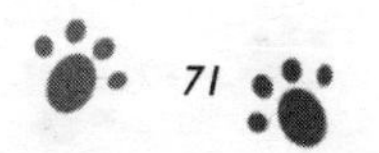

everyone started shouting at once. That sounded *seriously* interesting!

Mr Evans waved for quiet. "Very old bones," he added. "*Roman* ones, in fact. Now let's concentrate, shall we? We've got a lot to do."

Each table was given a different task. One group got Cliffside's first teachers to read about. Another got the men who built the school. The third group was in charge of sticking up the displays that the class had already made.

"You lot have got the bones," said Mr Evans, putting some papers down on Bella, Amber and Sophie's table.

"Cool, Mr Evans!" Bella gasped. She

exchanged high-fives with Amber. Sophie looked horrified.

"And the archaeologists," Mr Evans added. "They're the people who dug the bones up. Perhaps Sophie had better focus on them?"

"Thanks, Mr Evans," said Sophie in relief.

"Half an hour, everyone!" Mr Evans clapped his hands. "Coloured display sheets at the back of the class!"

"I can't believe you don't want to read stuff about the bones," Amber said to Sophie ten minutes later, as Bella cut out some of the articles and stuck them down on bright orange paper.

"This is more interesting," Sophie said stubbornly. She waved around her article about the archaeologists. "There were two men and one woman who worked on the site, digging up your icky bones. Look, here's a picture of them."

She waved the old picture at Bella and Amber. Bella gasped.

"Give me that!" she said, and snatched the picture.

"Hey!" Sophie began.

But Bella wasn't listening. She was staring at the caption under the photograph.

Archaeologists Nicholas Brown, Malcolm Fox and Clara Flynn dig up Sandmouth's history.

Bella was so excited when she met Suzi at the gates that she could hardly get her words out.

"Are you washing Archie today, Mum?" she tumbled out. "You usually do it on Tuesdays, right? I've seen a picture of Mr Flynn's wife! She was an archaeologist! She dug up a Roman under the school hall!"

"Slow down!" Suzi protested. "What Roman?"

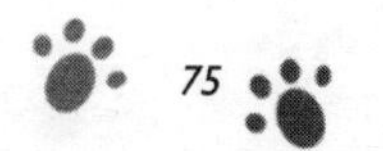

Bella explained. It was such a brilliant coincidence. She couldn't wait to tell Mr Flynn. He couldn't be grumpy about this. He just couldn't.

"I'm washing Archie at four o'clock again," said Suzi. "Want to come with me?"

Bella nodded. She glanced around. "Where's Louie?" she asked.

"Don't you remember?" Suzi said.

Bella was about to shake her head when she saw Louie's football team trooping out to the sports field. Oh yes.

Poor old Louie.

Mr Flynn was waiting as Bella and her mum

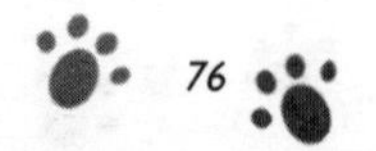

drove up and parked in his driveway.

"Sorry about last week," he said a little gruffly.

"Don't worry about it, Mr Flynn," said Suzi.

Archie wriggled as Suzi coaxed him into the bath. Bella had to hold the big dog still so Suzi could wash him. He was strong. Bella got soaked twice as Archie shook himself.

"Cup of tea?" said Mr Flynn when they had finished.

Bella glanced at her mum in surprise. Mr Flynn was inviting them in?

"We'd love to, but we have to collect Louie," said Suzi apologetically.

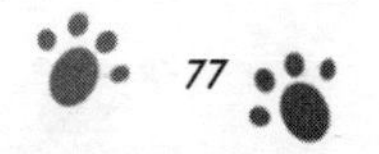

"Ah well," Mr Flynn said with a sniff. "You'd best get on then."

Bella decided to be brave. They were about to go, after all.

"Mr Flynn?" she said, as the old man handed twenty pounds to Suzi and prepared to go inside. "We're doing a project about my school. I saw a picture of your wife digging up some Roman bones before they built the hall."

Mr Flynn stood very still. Bella felt worried. Had she upset him?

"Those bones were Clara's best find," Mr Flynn said at last. "But they were bad news too. She lost a necklace I gave her, right down there in all the muck. Never found it again. When you take something out of the ground like that, perhaps you have to give something back."

"Are you sure you wouldn't like to come to my school's Summer Fair, Mr Flynn?" said Bella impulsively. "I'll describe the display we've done about your wife and the bones and everything. There's even going to be a dog show. You could enter Archie!"

"The school would love it," Suzi put in. "Especially as it's their fiftieth anniversary. It's this Saturday, at two o'clock."

"I'll think about it," said Mr Flynn reluctantly. "It might be good, visiting the place where Clara worked all those years ago."

And that was all he would say.

Seven

Purple!

The school playing field was covered in fluttering flags as Bella, her mum and her brother drove up to the gates in the van on Saturday morning.

"Dream Dogs, coming through!" Suzi called merrily out of her window.

Mr Evans opened the gates wide so the

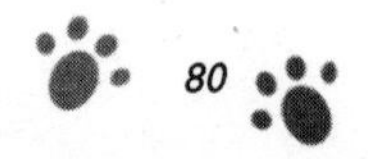

Dream Dogs van and trailer could fit through. They bumped over the grass and parked underneath a big chestnut tree. Bella was pleased that the dogs they were going to wash would get plenty of shade. It was really hot today.

"Nothing much to do yet," said Suzi, as Bella asked if her mum needed any help setting things up. "Why don't you take Pepper and go and have some fun?"

Bella got out of the van, put Pepper on his lead and ran to see Amber a little further down the field. Amber was helping her mum, Claire, to set up an Arts and Crafts stall.

"We're doing dip-dyeing," Amber explained,

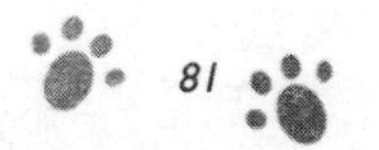

as Claire put up a clothesline at the back of the stall.

Bella looked at the little white squares of cloth that Amber was folding up. "What's that?" she asked curiously. She unfolded one of the pieces of cloth, before Amber whacked her hand and she folded it up again in a hurry.

"You fold the cloths, and dip the corners in these different colours," Amber explained. She pointed at the big bottles of dye that were lined up on the stall. "Then you unfold them and peg them up on our clothesline to dry. You get amazing patterns and colours. When they've dried, you can use them for anything. Hankies. Hats. Scarves. Whatever you like."

"It's a brilliant idea!" Bella said. She decided at once that she'd come and do a dip-dyed scarf for her mum a bit later on. "Down, Pepper!" she said as Pepper jumped up and nearly knocked over a big bottle of green dye.

Further down the field, Bella saw Louie with his friend Jamie. Jamie's dad was in charge of the bouncy castle. Both boys were climbing on the castle as it inflated, laughing and pushing each other.

"No bouncing yet, Louie!" Mrs Frost called, striding past with Charlie at her side. "The castle's not safe until it's fully inflated. We don't want any accidents today!"

Louie stuck his tongue out at Mrs Frost's back.

"Don't do that, Louie," Bella warned. "What if Frosty turns round and sees you?"

"I don't care," said Louie darkly. He still hadn't forgiven Mrs Frost for making him miss his first football match.

People were starting to pour through the gates. Music crackled through the loudspeakers that had been hung up in the trees. To Bella's delight, there were more dogs than she could ever have hoped for. Spaniels, Labradors, Jack Russells, and even a huge Great Dane! Pepper barked himself hoarse, sniffing all the dogs in his usual friendly way and nearly pulling Bella's arm off.

Bella ate some candy floss and dip-dyed a scarf. After playing with her friends, guessing the name of the giant teddy and stroking every dog she

could see, Bella headed back to the Dream Dogs trailer to help her mum. Louie was there, kicking his football against the wheel of the

trailer, but he stopped as soon as he saw Bella and started laughing, pointing at her hands.

"Bella, look at your fingers!" Suzi gasped.

Bella looked. Her hands had turned into rainbows! Red, purple and yellow splodges ran over her fingers and palms. It looked pretty cool.

"It was the dip-dyeing," she explained. "Don't worry, Claire said all the dyes are totally safe and wash off with soap and water. Have you been busy, Mum?"

"Most people have just been looking," Suzi said. "And asking me questions. Perhaps five pounds is a bit expensive?"

"Mrs Frost thought it would be OK," said

Bella. She licked a bit of sticky sugar off one red and purple finger. "Do you want me to go round and do some advertising?"

"Good idea," said Suzi. "I've done some leaflets. You can hand them out."

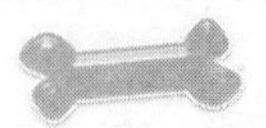

Bella wandered around, giving out leaflets to all the people with dogs.

"Wash your dog!" she called. "Only five pounds!"

After five minutes, she met Mrs Frost.

"Oh yes," said Mrs Frost, taking one of the leaflets as Bella fussed over Charlie. "I'll do that now."

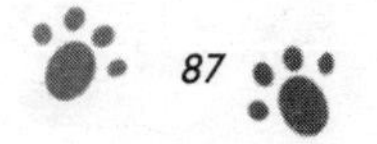

Bella noticed Louie and Jamie hanging close by. They were giggling about something. When Louie saw Bella looking, he stuck out his tongue and ran off with Jamie towards the dip-dyeing stall.

Sophie's mother Mrs Olowu was at a stand called 'Cliffside's Past', chatting to a man with 'Sandmouth Museum' written on his badge. Bella walked over to take a look.

"All of these things were found under the hall when the builders started clearing the site," Mrs Olowu told Bella. "Isn't it exciting?"

"The workers are finding more things all the time," said the man from the museum. "Roman pottery. A Saxon bead. Sandmouth Museum is giving the school some money for whatever they find. Not sure what this necklace was doing there though. It's not exactly ancient!"

Bella gazed at the shiny gold chain that lay among the broken bits of brick and pottery. A gold pendant hung from it. It was covered with bumps that Bella recognised as Braille – the written language for blind people. History rushed at her like a speeding train.

"Clara's necklace!" she gasped. "Oh, please, I know who this belongs to! Can you keep it safe until I get back?"

The man from the museum shrugged. "No problem," he said. "It's not going anywhere."

Bella ran back towards Dream Dogs. She hunted through the crowd. Had Mr Flynn and Archie come to the fair?

"Bella?"

Bella spun round. It was Amber.

"Our purple dye bottle's gone," Amber said. "Mum can't understand it. You didn't see anyone walking around with a bottle, did you?"

"You probably used it all up," said Bella,

forgetting about the necklace in her hand for a second.

Amber scratched her head. "We can't have," she said. "The whole purple bottle has disappeared, and there are hardly any purple cloths drying on the line."

Bella glanced back at the Dream Dogs trailer. There were one or two people there now, waiting their turn. She could see Mrs Frost at the front of the line. A wet Charlie was in the bathtub. Suzi upended a shampoo bottle over the Labradoodle's back, chatting to Mrs Frost as she worked.

Bella was nearly knocked off her feet as Jamie and Louie raced by, giggling madly. And

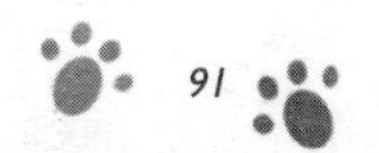

then she understood.

The way Louie had been hanging around Mrs Frost earlier. How Louie'd been going on for days about getting Frosty back for making him miss his football match. The missing dye bottle. It all added up to one thing.

Bella saw Charlie jump out of the bathtub and shake himself.

"Oh, my life!" screamed Suzi.

"Goodness," said Mrs Frost.

Bella clapped her hand to her mouth.

The creamy-white patches on Charlie's back and bottom were now a beautiful lilac.

Eight

An Announcement

"Mrs Frost, I'm so sorry!" Suzi said, over and over again.

Charlie looked amazing. He stood there smiling up at Mrs Frost, wagging his new purple tail, totally unfazed by all the attention he was getting. It looked like the white parts of him had been coloured in with Bella's purple gel pen that smelled of grapes.

"Goodness," said Mrs Frost again.

Bella felt weak. Frosty was going to go completely MAD. She caught sight of Louie and Jamie rolling around on the grass, clutching their tummies and howling with laughter. More people started moving across the playing field to see what the fuss was about.

"Wow!" Amber gasped, still standing beside Bella. "Is that Frosty's dog? Is he supposed to be that colour?"

"I think," said Bella, "we just found out where your mum's bottle of purple dye went."

"Purple dye in the *shampoo?*" Suzi shrieked.

"Mrs Frost, I'm so... I don't... LOUIE!!!"

"Hahahaha," squealed Louie and Jamie.

"Louie's in for it, big time," Bella said to Amber as Suzi marched over to where Louie and Jamie still lay helpless on the grass.

"Stop," called Mrs Frost.

Suzi froze. So did Louie and Jamie, and Bella and Amber. In fact, everyone on the playing field seemed to stop talking, all at once. Mrs Frost had that effect.

And then...

"I think Charlie looks wonderful," said Mrs Frost, with the broadest smile Bella had ever seen. "So original. He'll be the only purple Labradoodle in the country! I'm assuming it washes out eventually?"

Suzi looked at Claire. Claire nodded and laughed. "Oh yes, they're made from a hundred per cent natural ingredients and are completely harmless. Another shampoo and he'll be back to, er, normal!" she spluttered.

"Five pounds, did you say?" said Mrs Frost. She rummaged in her purse and pulled out two five-pound notes. "Let's make it ten."

People started rushing forward with their dogs.

"Do you do other colours?"

"Do you think my spaniel would suit green?"

"I don't believe it," Bella giggled, as a flood of people started lining up at the Dream Dogs trailer. "Everyone wants to dye their dogs! Why didn't I think of that?"

"Your mum could make thousands!" Amber gasped.

Although the idea of making that kind of money sounded tempting, Suzi shook her head. "Let's just stick to the usual, shall we?" she laughed. "I guarantee every dog here will look absolutely gorgeous after they've had the Dream Dogs treatment... just perhaps not quite so colourful!"

Something was cutting into Bella's hand. She looked down. The necklace winked up at her. And she remembered.

"Amber, have you seen an old man wearing dark glasses and carrying a white stick?" she said urgently. "He's got a big German shepherd dog with him. He's probably not here because he doesn't go out much, but we asked him to come and—"

"Do you mean him?" Amber asked, and pointed.

Mr Flynn was walking past the candy-floss

stand, holding on to Archie's harness. Mr Evans walked beside him.

"Here we are, sir," said Mr Evans, stopping at the crowded Dream Dogs trailer. "Bella!" he called. "This gentleman said you invited him to the fair?"

Bella took Mr Flynn's hand.

"Is that Bella?" said Mr Flynn.

"Yes," said Bella happily. "I'm really pleased that you came. I've got something for you."

She put the necklace into Mr Flynn's palm. Mr Flynn felt the gold links in the chain. He ran his finger over the bumps on the pendant. He smiled.

"So," he said. "It came back, did it? Well, well."

"The bumps," said Bella shyly. "What do they say?"

"Clara, of course," said Mr Flynn.

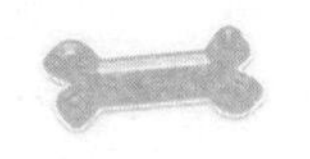

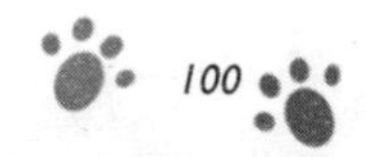

The fair was over. Stallholders were packing up their tables and counting their money.

"How did we do, Mum?" Bella asked.

Suzi wiped some soap bubbles off her nose and blew out her cheeks. "I've never been so busy," she laughed. "Look at all the pampered dogs in the field!"

Bella looked. She spotted a Labrador whose glossy black coat shone like satin, a bichon frise who was so fluffy he looked like a powder puff with legs and a snowy white West Highland terrier with a tiny tartan bow in her topknot. And there had been plenty of others too.

"We made three hundred and forty pounds!" Bella gasped, counting the money in their

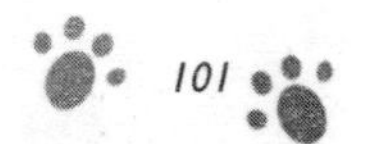

cashbox. "That's amazing!"

Pepper panted happily underneath the van. A blue rosette was pinned to his collar. He'd come second in his class at the dog show and was looking very pleased with himself.

"Can't I get out of the van now, Mum?" Louie said from the van window. "I'm bored."

"You stay there," said Suzi fiercely. "And you can say goodbye to your pocket money for the next three weeks."

"But Frosty *liked* it!" Louie moaned. "You wouldn't have done nearly so well if I hadn't put the dye in the shampoo!"

"OK, two weeks," said Suzi. "But you're staying in the van till we get home."

Mrs Frost came over. She wrote '£340' on her clipboard and smiled at Bella and Suzi. "A wonderful job," she said. "Well done."

Bella stroked Charlie's purple tail. The colour suited him.

Mrs Frost and Charlie moved across the field. Bella saw her stop to talk to Mr Flynn, who was sitting on a deckchair by the tea tent with Archie at his feet.

"Mrs Frost and Mr Flynn have been talking for ages," said Louie, out of the van window ten minutes later.

"They're probably talking about the work his wife did on the excavations," said Suzi as a group of people gathered around Mr Flynn.

At last, Mrs Frost walked over to the microphone. For some reason, she was holding Mr Flynn by the arm. Bella felt excited. They were going to find out how much money the fair had made!

"Attention, everyone!" Mrs Frost said.

The field fell quiet.

"Thank you all for your hard work today," said the head teacher. "We've had a wonderful fair. Money is still coming in, but I can tell you that we've raised nearly five thousand pounds. A magnificent effort!"

Everyone cheered and applauded. Bella did too. She felt so proud that Dream Dogs had helped contribute to the new roof fund. Everyone had worked so hard to raise as much money as possible and they weren't too far off reaching their ten thousand pound goal – just another five thousand to go! Bella didn't want to spoil such a lovely day by worrying about

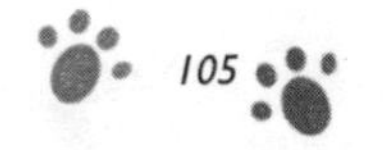

how they were going to raise that last part, so she concentrated on listening to her head teacher.

"Now, I'm going to hand you over to this gentleman here," Mrs Frost went on. "Mr Flynn has something rather wonderful to say."

Mrs Frost stepped aside. Archie guided Mr Flynn towards the microphone.

"My wife," began Mr Flynn down the microphone. He cleared his throat. "My wife, Clara Flynn, worked on the site here at Cliffside Primary. She dug up a Roman underneath your hall."

There were a few cheers.

"She also lost something," Mr Flynn continued.

He held up the little gold necklace. “I gave her this fifty years ago. It was found this week.”

There were more cheers. Bella clapped hard.

“I always think,” said Mr Flynn, “that when

you take something away, you give something back. My wife took away a Roman, and left a necklace in his place. Now I have the necklace back. So I thought to myself, what can I give in return?"

The crowd started murmuring.

"I thought about your hall," Mr Flynn continued. "It's where it all began, you see. And so I'm pleased to offer Cliffside Primary School the remaining five thousand pounds you need to help rebuild the roof. My only request is that the new hall is named after my wife. I hope that's all right?"

Bella sat down on the grass very suddenly. The air was full of the loudest cheers she'd ever heard. Pepper jumped on her lap and licked her nose.

"I think," Bella gasped, "that maybe we just had the best fair *ever*!"

Top tips from vets!

If you'd like your dog to have the Dream Dogs treatment, read our simple tips to keep them in tip-top condition.

- **Keep your dog's coat well groomed. Long-haired dogs should be brushed at least once a day, while short-haired dogs should be brushed about once or twice a week. Of course, you might have to do this more frequently if you take them out for a muddy walk!**
- **Make sure your dog doesn't get overweight by keeping them active and taking them for plenty of walks.**
- **Clipping your dog's nails will keep them looking their best. Untrimmed nails can make it uncomfortable for your dog when walking, so make sure it is part of their regular grooming routine. Ask your vet or dog groomer about how to do this.**
- **Ban bad breath by brushing your dog's teeth regularly. Use special toothbrushes and pet toothpastes, as well as specially designed foods, toys and chews.**
- **What you feed your dog affects their coat. Ask your vet what is best for your dog. For example, an older dog will have different needs than a puppy.**

The pupils at Cliffside Primary raised a lot of money at their school fair. If you would like to help PDSA by raising funds to help sick and injured pets visit www.pdsa.org.uk/petprotectors for fab fundraising tips and ideas.

for pets in need of vets

Take home all of the Dream Dogs

If you have it, tick it!